WILLIAM
SHAKESPEARE

THE COMEDY
OF ERRORS

Edited By William George Clark And John Glover

CLASSICS

Published 2024

FiNGERPRINT! CLASSICS
Prakash Books

Fingerprint Publishing
@FingerprintP
@fingerprintpublishingbooks
www.fingerprintpublishing.com

ISBN: 978 93 8993 103 7

William Shakespeare began his career as an actor, writer, and part owner of a playing company called the Lord Chamberlain's Men, later known as King's Men, in London. Often regarded as the 'Bard of Avon' he is one of the world's pre-eminent dramatists. Born and brought up in Stratford-upon-Avon, he married Anne Hathaway at the age of eighteen and they had three children—Susanna, and twins Hamnet and Judith. Though few records survive of his private life, he appeared to have retired to Stratford around 1613 where he died three years later.

His works still in existence, including some collaborations, consist of thirty-eight plays, one hundred and fifty-four sonnets, two long narrative poems, and several other verses. His plays are performed much more than any other playwright's and have been translated in almost all major languages. Most of his known works have been produced between 1589 and 1613. His early plays were mainly comedies and histories which remain regarded as some of the best works produced in these genres.

Shakespeare's plays are difficult to date. His early classical and Italianate comedies contain tight double plots and precise comic sequences giving way to the romantic atmosphere of his most acclaimed comedies in the mid-1590s. *The Comedy of Errors*, *The Two Gentlemen of Verona*, and *Love's Labour's Lost* are his early comedies. These were followed by *A Midsummer Night's Dream*, the play with which he achieved complete success in romantic comedy.

Based on *Menaechmi*, Plautus' greatest play, *The Comedy of Errors* is his shortest written comedy. It follows the story of two sets of identical twins who are separated during a shipwreck while they are still babies, and years later happen to be in the same town. A slapstick comedy of incident, this brilliantly crafted farce is a drama of mistaken identities, bafflement, joy, wordplay, and confusion. *The Comedy of Errors* is one of the only two Shakespearean plays— the other being *The Tempest*—which observe the unity of time (one of the three Aristotelian unities). It continues to be staged worldwide.

A Midsummer Night's Dream—a witty mixture of romance, fairy magic, and comic low life scenes—is one of Shakespeare's most delightful creations shortly before he turned to *Romeo and Juliet*. *Romeo and Juliet* is his most famous romantic tragedy of sexually charged adolescence, love, and death. It marks a departure from his earlier works and from others of the English Renaissance.

His plays demonstrate the expansiveness of his imagination and the extent of his learning. Shakespeare's sequence of great comedies continues with *Merchant of Venice*, *Much Ado About Nothing*, *As You Like It*, and *Twelfth Night*. Exploring the themes of bigotry, prejudice, justice, and humanity, *Merchant of Venice* is considered an anti-Semitic work. The play continues to remain one of his great comedies.

Shakespeare introduced prose comedy in the histories of the late 1590s—*Henry IV, Part I* and *Part II*, and *Henry V*—after the lyrical *Richard II. Julius Caesar* introduced a new kind of drama. Based on true events from Roman history, it is one of Shakespeare's most loved political tragedies.

Shakespeare wrote the so-called 'problem plays' in the early 17th century. *Measure for Measure*, *Troilus and Cressida*, and *All's Well that Ends Well* being a few of them. Until about 1608, he mainly wrote tragedies including *Hamlet*, *Othello*, *King Lear*, and *Macbeth*.

Othello is the story of the eponymous character who is a soldier in the service of the Venetian Republic. On instigation of his villainous ensign, Iago, Othello murders his beloved wife, Desdemona, only to find out later that she is innocent. An emotional drama of love, jealously, betrayal, revenge, and repentance, *Othello* reveals how fabricated lies and manipulation of evidences can lead to wrong judgement and suddenness of action, which ultimately result in the fall of a man.

Antony and Cleopatra and *Coriolanus*—his last major tragedies, contain some of his finest poetry. Shakespeare wrote tragicomedies, also known as romances, in his last phase. These include *Cymbeline*, *The Winter's Tale*, and *The Tempest*, as well as the collaboration *Pericles, Prince of Tyre*.

A true genius, Shakespeare's popular characters and plots are studied, performed, reinterpreted, and discussed till today. William Shakespeare, known as the English national poet, is considered the greatest dramatist of all time.

CHARACTERS OF THE PLAY*

SOLINUS†, Duke of Ephesus

AEGEON, a merchant of Syracuse

AEMILIA, wife to Aegeon, an abbess at Ephesus

ANTIPHOLUS‡ of Ephesus } twin brothers, and sons
ANTIPHOLUS of Syracuse } to Aegeon and Aemilia

DROMIO of Ephesus } twin brothers, and attendants
DROMIO of Syracuse } on the two Antipholuses

ADRIANA, wife to Antipholus of Ephesus

LUCIANA, her sister

BALTHAZAR, a merchant

ANGELO, a goldsmith

FIRST MERCHANT, friend to Antipholus of Syracuse

---

* DRAMATIS PERSONAE first given by Rowe.
† SOLINUS
‡ ANTIPHOLUS

SECOND MERCHANT, to whom Angelo is a debtor
PINCH, a schoolmaster
LUCE, servant to Adriana
A Courtesan
Gaoler, Officers, and other Attendants

SCENE:
EPHESUS

Act I

SCENE I. A HALL IN THE DUKE'S PALACE

Enter DUKE, AEGEON, Gaoler, Officers, *and other* Attendants

AEGEON

    Proceed, Solinus, to procure my fall,

    And by the doom of death end woes and all.

DUKE

    Merchant of Syracusa, plead no more;

    I am not partial to infringe our laws.

    The enmity and discord which of late

    Sprung from the rancorous outrage of your Duke

    To merchants, our well-dealing countrymen,

    Who, wanting guilders to redeem their lives,

    Have seal'd his rigorous statutes with their bloods,

    Excludes all pity from our threatening looks.

For, since the mortal and intestine jars
'Twixt thy seditious countrymen and us,
It hath in solemn synods been decreed,
Both by the Syracusians and ourselves,
To admit no traffic to our adverse towns.
Nay, more,
If any born at Ephesus be seen
At any Syracusian marts and fairs;
Again, if any Syracusian born
Come to the bay of Ephesus, he dies,
His goods confiscate to the Duke's dispose;
Unless a thousand marks be levied,
To quit the penalty and to ransom him.
Thy substance, valued at the highest rate,
Cannot amount unto a hundred marks;
Therefore by law thou art condemn'd to die.

AEGEON

Yet this my comfort: when your words are
done,
My woes end likewise with the evening sun.

DUKE

Well, Syracusian, say, in brief, the cause
Why thou departed'st from thy native home,
And for what cause thou camest to Ephesus.

AEGEON

A heavier task could not have been imposed
Than I to speak my griefs unspeakable.

Yet, that the world may witness that my end
Was wrought by nature, not by vile offence,
I'll utter what my sorrow gives me leave.
In Syracusa was I born; and wed
Unto a woman, happy but for me,
And by me, had not our hap been bad.
With her I lived in joy; our wealth increased
By prosperous voyages I often made
To Epidamnum; till my factor's death,
And the great care of goods at random left,
Drew me from kind embracements of my
 spouse,
From whom my absence was not six months
 old,
Before herself, almost at fainting under
The pleasing punishment that women bear,
Had made provision for her following me,
And soon and safe arrived where I was.
There had she not been long but she became
A joyful mother of two goodly sons;
And, which was strange, the one so like the
 other
As could not be distinguish'd but by names.
That very hour, and in the self-same inn,
A meaner woman was delivered
Of such a burden, male twins, both alike.
Those, for their parents were exceeding poor,

I bought, and brought up to attend my sons.
My wife, not meanly proud of two such boys,
Made daily motions for our home return.
Unwilling I agreed; alas! too soon
We came aboard.
A league from Epidamnum had we sail'd,
Before the always-wind-obeying deep
Gave any tragic instance of our harm.
But longer did we not retain much hope;
For what obscured light the heavens did grant
Did but convey unto our fearful minds
A doubtful warrant of immediate death;
Which though myself would gladly have embraced,
Yet the incessant weepings of my wife,
Weeping before for what she saw must come,
And piteous plainings of the pretty babes,
That mourn'd for fashion, ignorant what to fear,
Forced me to seek delays for them and me.
And this it was, for other means was none,
The sailors sought for safety by our boat,
And left the ship, then sinking-ripe, to us.
My wife, more careful for the latter-born,
Had fasten'd him unto a small spare mast,
Such as seafaring men provide for storms;
To him one of the other twins was bound,
Whilst I had been like heedful of the other.

The children thus disposed, my wife and I,
Fixing our eyes on whom our care was fix'd,
Fasten'd ourselves at either end the mast;
And floating straight, obedient to the stream,
Was carried towards Corinth, as we thought.
At length the sun, gazing upon the earth,
Dispersed those vapours that offended us;
And, by the benefit of his wished light,
The seas wax'd calm, and we discovered
Two ships from far making amain to us,
Of Corinth that, of Epidaurus this.
But ere they came—O, let me say no more!
Gather the sequel by that went before.

DUKE

Nay, forward, old man; do not break off so;
For we may pity, though not pardon thee.

AEGEON

O, had the gods done so, I had not now
Worthily term'd them merciless to us!
For, ere the ships could meet by twice five
        leagues,
We were encounter'd by a mighty rock;
Which being violently borne upon,
Our helpful ship was splitted in the midst;
So that, in this unjust divorce of us,
Fortune had left to both of us alike
What to delight in, what to sorrow for.

Her part, poor soul! seeming as burdened
With lesser weight, but not with lesser woe,
Was carried with more speed before the wind;
And in our sight they three were taken up
By fishermen of Corinth, as we thought.
At length, another ship had seized on us;
And, knowing whom it was their hap to save,
Gave healthful welcome to their shipwreck'd
    guests;
And would have reft the fishers of their prey,
Had not their bark been very slow of sail;
And therefore homeward did they bend their
    course.
Thus have you heard me sever'd from my bliss;
That by misfortunes was my life prolong'd,
To tell sad stories of my own mishaps.

DUKE

And, for the sake of them thou sorrowest for,
Do me the favour to dilate at full
What hath befall'n of them and thee till now.

AEGEON

My youngest boy, and yet my eldest care,
At eighteen years became inquisitive
After his brother, and importuned me
That his attendant—so his case was like,
Reft of his brother, but retain'd his name—
Might bear him company in the quest of him;

16

Whom whilst I labour'd of a love to see,
I hazarded the loss of whom I loved.
Five summers have I spent in furthest Greece,
Roaming clean through the bounds of Asia,
And, coasting homeward, came to Ephesus;
Hopeless to find, yet loath to leave unsought
Or that, or any place that harbours men.
But here must end the story of my life;
And happy were I in my timely death,
Could all my travels warrant me they live.

DUKE

Hapless Aegeon, whom the fates have mark'd
To bear the extremity of dire mishap!
Now, trust me, were it not against our laws,
Against my crown, my oath, my dignity,
Which princes, would they, may not disannul,
My soul should sue as advocate for thee.
But, though thou art adjudged to the death,
And passed sentence may not be recall'd
But to our honour's great disparagement,
Yet will I favour thee in what I can.
Therefore, merchant, I'll limit thee this day
To seek thy help by beneficial help.
Try all the friends thou hast in Ephesus;
Beg thou, or borrow, to make up the sum,
And live; if no, then thou art doom'd to die.
Gaoler, take him to thy custody.

GAOLER

I will, my lord.

AEGEON

Hopeless and helpless doth Aegeon wend,

But to procrastinate his lifeless end.

Exeunt

SCENE II. THE MART

Enter ANTIPHOLUS of Syracuse, DROMIO of
Syracuse, *and* First Merchant

FIRST MERCHANT

Therefore give out you are of Epidamnum,

Lest that your goods too soon be confiscate.

This very day a Syracusian merchant

Is apprehended for arrival here;

And, not being able to buy out his life,

According to the statute of the town,

Dies ere the weary sun set in the west.

There is your money that I had to keep.

ANTIPHOLUS OF SYRACUSE

Go bear it to the Centaur, where we host,

And stay there, Dromio, till I come to thee.

Within this hour it will be dinner-time.

Till that. I'll view the manners of the town,

Peruse the traders, gaze upon the buildings,

And then return, and sleep within mine inn;
For with long travel I am stiff and weary.
Get thee away.

DROMIO OF SYRACUSE

Many a man would take you at your word,
And go indeed, having so good a mean.

Exit

ANTIPHOLUS OF SYRACUSE

A trusty villain, sir; that very oft,
When I am dull with care and melancholy,
Lightens my humour with his merry jests.
What, will you walk with me about the town,
And then go to my inn, and dine with me?

FIRST MERCHANT

I am invited, sir, to certain merchants,
Of whom I hope to make much benefit;
I crave your pardon. Soon at five o'clock,
Please you, I'll meet with you upon the mart,
And afterward consort you till bed-time.
My present business calls me from you now.

ANTIPHOLUS OF SYRACUSE

Farewell till then. I will go lose myself,
And wander up and down to view the city.

FIRST MERCHANT

Sir, I commend you to your own content.

Exit

ANTIPHOLUS OF SYRACUSE

> He that commends me to mine own content
> Commends me to the thing I cannot get.
> I to the world am like a drop of water,
> That in the ocean seeks another drop;
> Who, falling there to find his fellow forth,
> Unseen, inquisitive, confounds himself.
> So I, to find a mother and a brother,
> In quest of them, unhappy, lose myself.

> _Enter_ DROMIO _of_ Ephesus

> Here comes the almanac of my true date.
> What now? How chance thou art return'd so soon?

DROMIO OF EPHESUS

> Return'd so soon! rather approach'd too late.
> The capon burns, the pig falls from the spit;
> The clock hath strucken twelve upon the bell;
> My mistress made it one upon my cheek.
> She is so hot, because the meat is cold;
> The meat is cold, because you come not home;
> You come not home, because you have no
>   stomach;
> You have no stomach, having broke your fast;
> But we, that know what 'tis to fast and pray,
> Are penitent for your default to-day.

ANTIPHOLUS OF SYRACUSE

> Stop in your wind, sir. Tell me this, I pray:
> Where have you left the money that I gave you?

DROMIO OF EPHESUS

    O, sixpence, that I had o' Wednesday last

    To pay the saddler for my mistress' crupper?

    The saddler had it, sir; I kept it not.

ANTIPHOLUS OF SYRACUSE

    I am not in a sportive humour now.

    Tell me, and dally not, where is the money?

    We being strangers here, how darest thou trust

    So great a charge from thine own custody?

DROMIO OF EPHESUS

    I pray you, jest, sir, as you sit at dinner.

    I from my mistress come to you in post;

    If I return, I shall be post indeed,

    For she will score your fault upon my pate.

    Methinks your maw, like mine, should be your
        clock,

    And strike you home without a messenger.

ANTIPHOLUS OF SYRACUSE

    Come, Dromio, come, these jests are out of
        season;

    Reserve them till a merrier hour than this.

    Where is the gold I gave in charge to thee?

DROMIO OF EPHESUS

    To me, sir? Why, you gave no gold to me.

ANTIPHOLUS OF SYRACUSE

    Come on, sir knave, have done your foolishness,

    And tell me how thou hast disposed thy charge.

DROMIO OF EPHESUS

>My charge was but to fetch you from the mart
>Home to your house, the Phœnix, sir, to dinner.
>My mistress and her sister stays for you.

ANTIPHOLUS OF SYRACUSE

>Now, as I am a Christian, answer me,
>In what safe place you have bestow'd my money;
>Or I shall break that merry sconce of yours,
>That stands on tricks when I am undisposed.
>Where is the thousand marks thou hadst of me?

DROMIO OF EPHESUS

>I have some marks of yours upon my pate,
>Some of my mistress' marks upon my shoulders;
>But not a thousand marks between you both.
>If I should pay your worship those again,
>Perchance you will not bear them patiently.

ANTIPHOLUS OF SYRACUSE

>Thy mistress' marks? What mistress, slave,
>hast thou?

DROMIO OF EPHESUS

>Your worship's wife, my mistress at the Phœnix;
>She that doth fast till you come home to dinner,
>And prays that you will hie you home to dinner.

ANTIPHOLUS OF SYRACUSE

>What, wilt thou flout me thus unto my face,
>Being forbid? There, take you that, sir knave.

>>*He beats Dromio*

DROMIO OF EPHESUS

> What mean you, sir? For God's sake, hold your
>> hands!
> Nay, an you will not, sir, I'll take my heels.

Exit

ANTIPHOLUS OF SYRACUSE

> Upon my life, by some device or other
> The villain is o'er-raught of all my money.
> They say this town is full of cozenage;
> As, nimble jugglers that deceive the eye,
> Dark-working sorcerers that change the mind.
> Soul-killing witches that deform the body,
> Disguised cheaters, prating mountebanks,
> And many such-like liberties of sin.
> If it prove so, I will be gone the sooner.
> I'll to the Centaur, to go seek this slave.
> I greatly fear my money is not safe.

Exit

Act II

SCENE I. THE HOUSE OF ANTIPHOLUS OF EPHESUS

Enter ADRIANA *and* LUCIANA

ADRIANA

Neither my husband nor the slave return'd,
That in such haste I sent to seek his master!
Sure, Luciana, it is two o'clock.

LUCIANA

Perhaps some merchant hath invited him,
And from the mart he's somewhere gone to
    dinner.
Good sister, let us dine, and never fret.
A man is master of his liberty.
Time is their master; and when they see time,
They'll go or come. If so, be patient, sister.

ADRIANA

Why should their liberty than ours be more?

LUCIANA

Because their business still lies out o' door.

ADRIANA

Look, when I serve him so, he takes it ill.

LUCIANA

O, know he is the bridle of your will.

ADRIANA

There's none but asses will be bridled so.

LUCIANA

Why, headstrong liberty is lash'd with woe.
There's nothing situate under heaven's eye
But hath his bound, in earth, in sea, in sky.
The beasts, the fishes, and the winged fowls,
Are their males' subjects and at their controls.
Men, more divine, the masters of all these,
Lords of the wide world and wild watery seas,
Indued with intellectual sense and souls,
Of more pre-eminence than fish and fowls,
Are masters to their females, and their lords.
Then let your will attend on their accords.

ADRIANA

This servitude makes you to keep unwed.

LUCIANA

Not this, but troubles of the marriage-bed.

ADRIANA

But, were you wedded, you would bear some
sway.

LUCIANA

Ere I learn love, I'll practise to obey.

ADRIANA

How if your husband start some otherwhere?

LUCIANA

Till he come home again, I would forbear.

ADRIANA

Patience unmoved! No marvel though she
   pause;

They can be meek that have no other cause.

A wretched soul, bruised with adversity,

We bid be quiet when we hear it cry;

But were we burden'd with like weight of pain,

As much, or more, we should ourselves
   complain.

So thou, that hast no unkind mate to grieve thee,

With urging helpless patience wouldst relieve
   me;

But, if thou live to see like right bereft,

This fool-begg'd patience in thee will be left.

LUCIANA

Well, I will marry one day, but to try.

Here comes your man; now is your husband
   nigh.

   Enter DROMIO of Ephesus

ADRIANA

Say, is your tardy master now at hand?

DROMIO OF EPHESUS

Nay, he's at two hands with me, and that my two
ears can witness.

ADRIANA

Say, didst thou speak with him? Know'st thou
his mind?

DROMIO OF EPHESUS

Ay, ay, he told his mind upon mine ear.
Beshrew his hand, I scarce could understand it.

LUCIANA

Spake he so doubtfully, thou couldst not feel
his meaning?

DROMIO OF EPHESUS

Nay, he struck so plainly, I could too well feel
his blows; and withal so doubtfully, that I
could scarce understand them.

ADRIANA

But say, I prithee, is he coming home?
It seems he hath great care to please his wife.

DROMIO OF EPHESUS

Why, mistress, sure my master is horn-mad.

ADRIANA

Horn-mad, thou villain!

DROMIO OF EPHESUS

I mean not cuckold-mad;
But, sure, he is stark mad.
When I desired him to come home to dinner,

He ask'd me for a thousand marks in gold.

''Tis dinner-time,' quoth I; 'My gold!' quoth he.

'Your meat doth burn,' quoth I; 'My gold!'
    quoth he.

'Will you come home?' quoth I; 'My gold!'
    quoth he,

'Where is the thousand marks I gave thee,
    villain?'

'The pig,' quoth I, 'is burn'd;' 'My gold!' quoth
    he.

'My mistress, sir,' quoth I; 'Hang up thy mistress!

I know not thy mistress; out on thy mistress!'

LUCIANA

Quoth who?

DROMIO OF EPHESUS

Quoth my master.

'I know,' quoth he, 'no house, no wife, no
    mistress.'

So that my errand, due unto my tongue,

I thank him, I bare home upon my shoulders;

For, in conclusion, he did beat me there.

ADRIANA

Go back again, thou slave, and fetch him
home.

DROMIO OF EPHESUS

Go back again, and be new-beaten home?

For God's sake, send some other messenger.

ADRIANA

Back, slave, or I will break thy pate across.

DROMIO OF EPHESUS

And he will bless that cross with other beating,

Between you I shall have a holy head.

ADRIANA

Hence, prating peasant! fetch thy master home.

She beats Dromio

DROMIO OF EPHESUS

Am I so round with you as you with me,

That like a football you do spurn me thus?

You spurn me hence, and he will spurn me hither.

If I last in this service, you must case me in
leather.

Exit

LUCIANA

Fie, how impatience lowereth in your face!

ADRIANA

His company must do his minions grace,

Whilst I at home starve for a merry look.

Hath homely age the alluring beauty took

From my poor cheek? Then he hath wasted it.

Are my discourses dull? barren my wit?

If voluble and sharp discourse be marr'd,

Unkindness blunts it more than marble hard.

Do their gay vestments his affections bait?

That's not my fault; he's master of my state.

What ruins are in me that can be found,
By him not ruin'd? Then is he the ground
Of my defeatures. My decayed fair
A sunny look of his would soon repair.
But, too unruly deer, he breaks the pale,
And feeds from home; poor I am but his stale.

LUCIANA

Self-harming jealousy! fie, beat it hence!

ADRIANA

Unfeeling fools can with such wrongs dispense.
I know his eye doth homage otherwhere;
Or else what lets it but he would be here?
Sister, you know he promised me a chain;
Would that alone, alone he would detain,
So he would keep fair quarter with his bed!
I see the jewel best enamelled
Will lose his beauty; yet the gold bides still,
That others touch, and often touching will
Wear gold, and no man that hath a name,
By falsehood and corruption doth it shame.
Since that my beauty cannot please his eye,
I'll weep what's left away, and weeping die.

LUCIANA

How many fond fools serve mad jealousy!

Exeunt

SCENE II. A PUBLIC PLACE

Enter ANTIPHOLUS of Syracuse

ANTIPHOLUS OF SYRACUSE

    The gold I gave to Dromio is laid up

    Safe at the Centaur; and the heedful slave

    Is wander'd forth, in care to seek me out

    By computation and mine host's report.

    I could not speak with Dromio since at first

    I sent him from the mart. See, here he comes.

        Enter DROMIO of Syracuse

    How now, sir! Is your merry humour alter'd?

    As you love strokes, so jest with me again.

    You know no Centaur? You receiv'd no gold?

    Your mistress sent to have me home to dinner?

    My house was at the Phœnix? Wast thou mad,

    That thus so madly thou didst answer me?

DROMIO OF SYRACUSE

    What answer, sir? When spake I such a word?

ANTIPHOLUS OF SYRACUSE

    Even now, even here, not half an hour since.

DROMIO OF SYRACUSE

    I did not see you since you sent me hence,

    Home to the Centaur, with the gold you gave

      me.

ANTIPHOLUS OF SYRACUSE

    Villain, thou didst deny the gold's receipt,

And told'st me of a mistress and a dinner;

For which, I hope, thou felt'st I was displeased.

DROMIO OF SYRACUSE

I am glad to see you in this merry vein.

What means this jest? I pray you, master, tell me.

ANTIPHOLUS OF SYRACUSE

Yea, dost thou jeer and flout me in the teeth?

Think'st thou I jest? Hold, take thou that, and
that.

Beating him

DROMIO OF SYRACUSE

Hold, sir, for God's sake! now your jest is earnest.

Upon what bargain do you give it me?

ANTIPHOLUS OF SYRACUSE

Because that I familiarly sometimes

Do use you for my fool, and chat with you,

Your sauciness will jest upon my love,

And make a common of my serious hours.

When the sun shines let foolish gnats make sport,

But creep in crannies when he hides his beams.

If you will jest with me, know my aspect,

And fashion your demeanour to my looks,

Or I will beat this method in your sconce.

DROMIO OF SYRACUSE

Sconce call you it? So you would leave
battering, I had rather have it a head. An you
use these blows long, I must get a sconce for

my head, and insconce it too; or else I shall
seek my wit in my shoulders. But, I pray, sir,
why am I beaten?

ANTIPHOLUS OF SYRACUSE

Dost thou not know?

DROMIO OF SYRACUSE

Nothing, sir, but that I am beaten.

ANTIPHOLUS OF SYRACUSE

Shall I tell you why?

DROMIO OF SYRACUSE

Ay, sir, and wherefore; for they say every why
hath a wherefore.

ANTIPHOLUS OF SYRACUSE

Why, first—for flouting me; and then,
wherefore—
For urging it the second time to me.

DROMIO OF SYRACUSE

Was there ever any man thus beaten out of
season,
When in the why and the wherefore is neither
rhyme nor reason?
Well, sir, I thank you.

ANTIPHOLUS OF SYRACUSE

Thank me, sir! for what?

DROMIO OF SYRACUSE

Marry, sir, for this something that you gave me
for nothing.

ANTIPHOLUS OF SYRACUSE

I'll make you amends next, to give you nothing for something. But say, sir, is it dinner-time?

DROMIO OF SYRACUSE

No, sir. I think the meat wants that I have.

ANTIPHOLUS OF SYRACUSE

In good time, sir; what's that?

DROMIO OF SYRACUSE

Basting.

ANTIPHOLUS OF SYRACUSE

Well, sir, then 'twill be dry.

DROMIO OF SYRACUSE

If it be, sir, I pray you, eat none of it.

ANTIPHOLUS OF SYRACUSE

Your reason?

DROMIO OF SYRACUSE

Lest it make you choleric, and purchase me another dry basting.

ANTIPHOLUS OF SYRACUSE

Well, sir, learn to jest in good time. There's a time for all things.

DROMIO OF SYRACUSE

I durst have denied that, before you were so choleric.

ANTIPHOLUS OF SYRACUSE

By what rule, sir?

DROMIO OF SYRACUSE

Marry, sir, by a rule as plain as the plain bald pate of Father Time himself.

ANTIPHOLUS OF SYRACUSE

Let's hear it.

DROMIO OF SYRACUSE

There's no time for a man to recover his hair that grows bald by nature.

ANTIPHOLUS OF SYRACUSE

May he not do it by fine and recovery?

DROMIO OF SYRACUSE

Yes, to pay a fine for a periwig, and recover the lost hair of another man.

ANTIPHOLUS OF SYRACUSE

Why is Time such a niggard of hair, being, as it is, so plentiful an excrement?

DROMIO OF SYRACUSE

Because it is a blessing that he bestows on beasts, and what he hath scanted men in hair, he hath given them in wit.

ANTIPHOLUS OF SYRACUSE

Why, but there's many a man hath more hair than wit.

DROMIO OF SYRACUSE

Not a man of those but he hath the wit to lose his hair.

ANTIPHOLUS OF SYRACUSE

Why, thou didst conclude hairy men plain dealers without wit.

DROMIO OF SYRACUSE

The plainer dealer, the sooner lost. Yet he loseth it in a kind of jollity.

ANTIPHOLUS OF SYRACUSE

For what reason?

DROMIO OF SYRACUSE

For two; and sound ones too.

ANTIPHOLUS OF SYRACUSE

Nay, not sound, I pray you.

DROMIO OF SYRACUSE

Sure ones, then.

ANTIPHOLUS OF SYRACUSE

Nay, not sure, in a thing falsing.

DROMIO OF SYRACUSE

Certain ones, then.

ANTIPHOLUS OF SYRACUSE

Name them.

DROMIO OF SYRACUSE

The one, to save the money that he spends in trimming; the other, that at dinner they should not drop in his porridge.

ANTIPHOLUS OF SYRACUSE

You would all this time have proved there is no time for all things.

DROMIO OF SYRACUSE

Marry, and did, sir; namely, no time to recover
hair lost by nature.

ANTIPHOLUS OF SYRACUSE

But your reason was not substantial, why there
is no time to recover.

DROMIO OF SYRACUSE

Thus I mend it: Time himself is bald, and
therefore to the world's end will have bald
followers.

ANTIPHOLUS OF SYRACUSE

I knew 'twould be a bald conclusion.

But, soft! who wafts us yonder?

Enter ADRIANA *and* LUCIANA

ADRIANA

Ay, ay, Antipholus, look strange and frown.

Some other mistress hath thy sweet aspects;

I am not Adriana nor thy wife.

The time was once when thou unurged wouldst
vow

That never words were music to thine ear,

That never object pleasing in thine eye,

That never touch well welcome to thy hand,

That never meat sweet-savour'd in thy taste,

Unless I spake, or look'd, or touch'd, or carved
to thee.

How comes it now, my husband, O, how comes it,

That thou art then estranged from thyself?
Thyself I call it, being strange to me,
That, undividable, incorporate,
Am better than thy dear self's better part.
Ah, do not tear away thyself from me!
For know, my love, as easy mayst thou fall
A drop of water in the breaking gulf,
And take unmingled thence that drop again,
Without addition or diminishing,
As take from me thyself, and not me too.
How dearly would it touch thee to the quick,
Shouldst thou but hear I were licentious,
And that this body, consecrate to thee,
By ruffian lust should be contaminate!
Wouldst thou not spit at me and spurn at me,
And hurl the name of husband in my face,
And tear the stain'd skin off my harlot brow,
And from my false hand cut the wedding ring,
And break it with a deep-divorcing vow?
I know thou canst; and therefore see thou do it.
I am possess'd with an adulterate blot;
My blood is mingled with the crime of lust;
For if we two be one, and thou play false,
I do digest the poison of thy flesh,
Being strumpeted by thy contagion.
Keep, then, fair league and truce with thy true bed;
I live distain'd, thou undishonoured.

ANTIPHOLUS OF SYRACUSE

> Plead you to me, fair dame? I know you not.
> In Ephesus I am but two hours old,
> As strange unto your town as to your talk;
> Who, every word by all my wit being scann'd,
> Wants wit in all one word to understand.

LUCIANA

> Fie, brother! how the world is changed with
> you!
> When were you wont to use my sister thus?
> She sent for you by Dromio home to dinner.

ANTIPHOLUS OF SYRACUSE

> By Dromio?

DROMIO OF SYRACUSE

> By me?

ADRIANA

> By thee; and this thou didst return from him,
> That he did buffet thee, and, in his blows,
> Denied my house for his, me for his wife.

ANTIPHOLUS OF SYRACUSE

> Did you converse, sir, with this gentlewoman?
> What is the course and drift of your compact?

DROMIO OF SYRACUSE

> I, sir? I never saw her till this time.

ANTIPHOLUS OF SYRACUSE

> Villain, thou liest; for even her very words
> Didst thou deliver to me on the mart.

DROMIO OF SYRACUSE

I never spake with her in all my life.

ANTIPHOLUS OF SYRACUSE

How can she thus, then, call us by our names,

Unless it be by inspiration.

ADRIANA

How ill agrees it with your gravity

To counterfeit thus grossly with your slave,

Abetting him to thwart me in my mood!

Be it my wrong you are from me exempt,

But wrong not that wrong with a more
contempt.

Come, I will fasten on this sleeve of thine.

Thou art an elm, my husband, I a vine,

Whose weakness, married to thy stronger state,

Makes me with thy strength to communicate.

If aught possess thee from me, it is dross,

Usurping ivy, brier, or idle moss;

Who, all for want of pruning, with intrusion

Infect thy sap, and live on thy confusion.

ANTIPHOLUS OF SYRACUSE

To me she speaks; she moves me for her theme.

What, was I married to her in my dream?

Or sleep I now, and think I hear all this?

What error drives our eyes and ears amiss?

Until I know this sure uncertainty,

I'll entertain the offer'd fallacy.

LUCIANA

Dromio, go bid the servants spread for dinner.

DROMIO OF SYRACUSE

O, for my beads! I cross me for a sinner.

This is the fairy land;—O spite of spites!

We talk with goblins, owls, and sprites.

If we obey them not, this will ensue,

They'll suck our breath, or pinch us black and
blue.

LUCIANA

Why pratest thou to thyself, and answer'st not?

Dromio, thou drone, thou snail, thou slug, thou
sot!

DROMIO OF SYRACUSE

I am transformed, master, am I not?

ANTIPHOLUS OF SYRACUSE

I think thou art in mind, and so am I.

DROMIO OF SYRACUSE

Nay, master, both in mind and in my shape.

ANTIPHOLUS OF SYRACUSE

Thou hast thine own form.

DROMIO OF SYRACUSE

No, I am an ape.

LUCIANA

If thou art chang'd to aught, 'tis to an ass.

DROMIO OF SYRACUSE

'Tis true; she rides me, and I long for grass.

'Tis so, I am an ass; else it could never be
But I should know her as well as she knows me.

ADRIANA

Come, come, no longer will I be a fool,
To put the finger in the eye and weep,
Whilst man and master laughs my woes to
scorn.
Come, sir, to dinner. Dromio, keep the gate.
Husband, I'll dine above with you to-day,
And shrive you of a thousand idle pranks.
Sirrah, if any ask you for your master,
Say he dines forth, and let no creature enter.
Come, sister. Dromio, play the porter well.

ANTIPHOLUS OF SYRACUSE

Am I in earth, in heaven, or in hell?
Sleeping or waking? mad or well-advised?
Known unto these, and to myself disguised!
I'll say as they say, and persever so,
And in this mist at all adventures go.

DROMIO OF SYRACUSE

Master, shall I be porter at the gate?

ADRIANA

Ay; and let none enter, lest I break your pate.

LUCIANA

Come, come, Antipholus, we dine too late.

Exeunt

Act III

Scene I. BEFORE THE HOUSE OF ANTIPHOLUS OF EPHESUS

Enter ANTIPHOLUS of Ephesus, DROMIO of Ephesus, ANGELO, *and* BALTHAZAR

ANTIPHOLUS OF EPHESUS

Good Signior Angelo, you must excuse us all;
My wife is shrewish when I keep not hours.
Say that I linger'd with you at your shop
To see the making of her carcanet,
And that to-morrow you will bring it home.
But here's a villain that would face me down
He met me on the mart, and that I beat him,
And charged him with a thousand marks in
    gold,
And that I did deny my wife and house.
Thou drunkard, thou, what didst thou mean by
    this?

DROMIO OF EPHESUS

Say what you will, sir, but I know what I know;
That you beat me at the mart, I have your hand
   to show.
If the skin were parchment, and the blows you
   gave were ink,
Your own handwriting would tell you what I
   think.

ANTIPHOLUS OF EPHESUS

I think thou art an ass.

DROMIO OF EPHESUS

Marry, so it doth appear
By the wrongs I suffer, and the blows I bear.
I should kick, being kick'd; and, being at that pass,
You would keep from my heels, and beware of
   an ass.

ANTIPHOLUS OF EPHESUS

You're sad, Signior Balthazar. Pray God our cheer
May answer my good will and your good
   welcome here.

BALTHASAR

I hold your dainties cheap, sir, and your
   welcome dear.

ANTIPHOLUS OF EPHESUS

O, Signior Balthazar, either at flesh or fish,
A table full of welcome makes scarce one
   dainty dish.

BALTHASAR

Good meat, sir, is common; that every churl
affords.

ANTIPHOLUS OF EPHESUS

And welcome more common; for that's
nothing but words.

BALTHASAR

Small cheer and great welcome makes a merry
feast.

ANTIPHOLUS OF EPHESUS

Ay to a niggardly host and more sparing guest.

But though my cates be mean, take them in
good part;

Better cheer may you have, but not with better
heart.

But, soft! my door is lock'd. Go bid them let us in.

DROMIO OF EPHESUS

Maud, Bridget, Marian, Cicely, Gillian, Ginn!

DROMIO OF SYRACUSE [*Within*]

Mome, malthorse, capon, coxcomb, idiot,
patch!

Either get thee from the door, or sit down at
the hatch.

Dost thou conjure for wenches, that thou call'st
for such store,

When one is one too many? Go get thee from
the door,

DROMIO OF EPHESUS

What patch is made our porter? My master stays
in the street.

DROMIO OF SYRACUSE [*Within*]

Let him walk from whence he came, lest he
catch cold on's feet.

ANTIPHOLUS OF EPHESUS

Who talks within there? Ho, open the door!

DROMIO OF SYRACUSE [*Within*]

Right, sir; I'll tell you when, an you'll tell me
wherefore.

ANTIPHOLUS OF EPHESUS

Wherefore? For my dinner. I have not dined
to-day.

DROMIO OF SYRACUSE [*Within*]

Nor to-day here you must not; come again
when you may.

ANTIPHOLUS OF EPHESUS

What art thou that keepest me out from the
house I owe?

DROMIO OF SYRACUSE [*Within*]

The porter for this time, sir, and my name is
Dromio.

DROMIO OF EPHESUS

O villain, thou hast stolen both mine office and
my name!

The one ne'er got me credit, the other mickle
    blame.

If thou hadst been Dromio to-day in my place,

Thou wouldst have changed thy face for a
    name, or thy name for an ass.

LUCE [*Within*]

O What a coil is there, Dromio? Who are those
at the gate?

DROMIO OF EPHESUS

O Let my master in, Luce.

LUCE [*Within*]

O Faith, no; he comes too late;

And so tell your master.

DROMIO OF EPHESUS

O O Lord, I must laugh!

Have at you with a proverb: shall I set in my
staff?

LUCE [*Within*]

O Have at you with another; that's—When? Can
you tell?

DROMIO OF SYRACUSE [*Within*]

O If thy name be call'd Luce, Luce, thou hast
answer'd him well.

ANTIPHOLUS OF EPHESUS

O Do you hear, you minion? you'll let us in, I
hope?

LUCE [*Within*]

I thought to have ask'd you.

DROMIO OF SYRACUSE [*Within*]

And you said no.

DROMIO OF EPHESUS

So, come, help. Well struck! There was blow for blow.

ANTIPHOLUS OF EPHESUS

Thou baggage, let me in.

LUCE [*Within*]

Can you tell for whose sake?

DROMIO OF EPHESUS

Master, knock the door hard.

LUCE [*Within*]

Let him knock till it ache.

ANTIPHOLUS OF EPHESUS

You'll cry for this, minion, if I beat the door down.

LUCE [*Within*]

What needs all that, and a pair of stocks in the town?

ADRIANA [*Within*]

Who is that at the door that keeps all this noise?

DROMIO OF SYRACUSE [*Within*]

By my troth, your town is troubled with unruly boys.

ANTIPHOLUS OF EPHESUS

Are you, there, wife? You might have come
before.

ADRIANA [*Within*]

Your wife, sir knave! go get you from the
door.

Exit with Luce

DROMIO OF EPHESUS

If you went in pain, master, this 'knave' would
go sore.

ANGELO

Here is neither cheer, sir, nor welcome. We
would fain have either.

BALTHASAR

In debating which was best, we shall part with
neither.

DROMIO OF EPHESUS

They stand at the door, master; bid them
welcome hither.

ANTIPHOLUS OF EPHESUS

There is something in the wind, that we cannot
get in.

DROMIO OF EPHESUS

You would say so, master, if your garments
were thin.

Your cake here is warm within; you stand here
in the cold.

It would make a man mad as a buck, to be so
    bought and sold.

ANTIPHOLUS OF EPHESUS

Go fetch me something. I'll break ope the gate.

DROMIO OF SYRACUSE [*Within*]

Break any breaking here, and I'll break your
    knave's pate.

DROMIO OF EPHESUS

A man may break a word with you, sir; and
    words are but wind;

Ay, and break it in your face, so he break it not
    behind.

DROMIO OF SYRACUSE [*Within*]

It seems thou want'st breaking. Out upon thee,
    hind!

DROMIO OF EPHESUS

Here's too much 'out upon thee!' I pray thee, let
    me in.

DROMIO OF SYRACUSE [*Within*]

Ay, when fowls have no feathers, and fish have
    no fin.

ANTIPHOLUS OF EPHESUS

Well, I'll break in. Go borrow me a crow.

DROMIO OF EPHESUS

A crow without feather? Master, mean you so?

For a fish without a fin, there's a fowl without
    a feather.

If a crow help us in, sirrah, we'll pluck a crow
    together.

ANTIPHOLUS OF EPHESUS

Go get thee gone; fetch me an iron crow.

BALTHASAR

Have patience, sir; O, let it not be so!

Herein you war against your reputation,

And draw within the compass of suspect

Th' unviolated honour of your wife.

Once this—your long experience of her
    wisdom,

Her sober virtue, years, and modesty,

Plead on her part some cause to you unknown;

And doubt not, sir, but she will well excuse

Why at this time the doors are made against
    you.

Be ruled by me. Depart in patience,

And let us to the Tiger all to dinner;

And about evening come yourself alone

To know the reason of this strange restraint.

If by strong hand you offer to break in

Now in the stirring passage of the day,

A vulgar comment will be made of it,

And that supposed by the common rout

Against your yet ungalled estimation,

That may with foul intrusion enter in,

And dwell upon your grave when you are dead;

53

For slander lives upon succession,
For ever housed where it gets possession.
ANTIPHOLUS OF EPHESUS
You have prevail'd. I will depart in quiet,
And, in despite of mirth, mean to be merry.
I know a wench of excellent discourse,
Pretty and witty; wild, and yet, too, gentle.
There will we dine. This woman that I mean,
My wife—but, I protest, without desert—
Hath oftentimes upbraided me withal.
To her will we to dinner. [*To* ANGELO] Get you home,
And fetch the chain; by this I know 'tis made.
Bring it, I pray you, to the Porpentine;
For there's the house. That chain will I bestow—
Be it for nothing but to spite my wife—
Upon mine hostess there. Good sir, make haste.
Since mine own doors refuse to entertain me,
I'll knock elsewhere, to see if they'll disdain me.
ANGELO
I'll meet you at that place some hour hence.
ANTIPHOLUS OF EPHESUS
Do so. This jest shall cost me some expense.

Exeunt

SCENE II. THE SAME

Enter LUCIANA *and* ANTIPHOLUS of Syracuse.

LUCIANA

 And may it be that you have quite forgot

 A husband's office? Shall, Antipholus,

 Even in the spring of love, thy love-springs rot?

 Shall love, in building, grow so ruinous?

 If you did wed my sister for her wealth,

 Then for her wealth's sake use her with more
   kindness;

 Or if you like elsewhere, do it by stealth;

 Muffle your false love with some show of
   blindness.

 Let not my sister read it in your eye;

 Be not thy tongue thy own shame's orator;

 Look sweet, speak fair, become disloyalty;

 Apparel vice like virtue's harbinger;

 Bear a fair presence, though your heart be
   tainted;

 Teach sin the carriage of a holy saint;

 Be secret-false: what need she be acquainted?

 What simple thief brags of his own attaint?

 'Tis double wrong, to truant with your bed,

 And let her read it in thy looks at board.

 Shame hath a bastard fame, well managed;

 Ill deeds are doubled with an evil word.

Alas, poor women! make us but believe,
Being compact of credit, that you love us;
Though others have the arm, show us the
sleeve;
We in your motion turn, and you may move us.
Then, gentle brother, get you in again;
Comfort my sister, cheer her, call her wife.
'Tis holy sport, to be a little vain,
When the sweet breath of flattery conquers strife.

ANTIPHOLUS OF SYRACUSE
Sweet mistress—what your name is else, I
know not,
Nor by what wonder you do hit of mine—
Less in your knowledge and your grace you
show not
Than our earth's wonder; more than earth
divine.
Teach me, dear creature, how to think and
speak;
Lay open to my earthy-gross conceit,
Smother'd in errors, feeble, shallow, weak,
The folded meaning of your words' deceit.
Against my soul's pure truth why labour you
To make it wander in an unknown field?
Are you a god? Would you create me new?
Transform me, then, and to your power I'll
yield.

But if that I am I, then well I know
Your weeping sister is no wife of mine,
Nor to her bed no homage do I owe.
Far more, far more to you do I decline.
O, train me not, sweet mermaid, with thy note,
To drown me in thy sister flood of tears.
Sing, siren, for thyself, and I will dote.
Spread o'er the silver waves thy golden hairs,
And as a bed I'll take them, and there lie;
And, in that glorious supposition, think
He gains by death that hath such means to die.
Let Love, being light, be drowned if she sink!

LUCIANA

What, are you mad, that you do reason so?

ANTIPHOLUS OF SYRACUSE

Not mad, but mated; how, I do not know.

LUCIANA

It is a fault that springeth from your eye.

ANTIPHOLUS OF SYRACUSE

For gazing on your beams, fair sun, being by.

LUCIANA

Gaze where you should, and that will clear your sight.

ANTIPHOLUS OF SYRACUSE

As good to wink, sweet love, as look on night.

LUCIANA

Why call you me love? Call my sister so.

ANTIPHOLUS OF SYRACUSE

    Thy sister's sister.

LUCIANA

    That's my sister.

ANTIPHOLUS OF SYRACUSE

    No;

    It is thyself, mine own self's better part,

    Mine eye's clear eye, my dear heart's dearer
        heart,

    My food, my fortune, and my sweet hope's aim,

    My sole earth's heaven, and my heaven's claim.

LUCIANA

    All this my sister is, or else should be.

ANTIPHOLUS OF SYRACUSE

    Call thyself sister, sweet, for I am thee.

    Thee will I love, and with thee lead my life.

    Thou hast no husband yet, nor I no wife.

    Give me thy hand.

LUCIANA

    O, soft, sir! hold you still.

    I'll fetch my sister, to get her good will.

Exit

Enter DROMIO of Syracuse

ANTIPHOLUS OF SYRACUSE

    Why, how now, Dromio! where runn'st thou
    so fast?

DROMIO OF SYRACUSE

Do you know me, sir? Am I Dromio? Am I your man? Am I myself?

ANTIPHOLUS OF SYRACUSE

Thou art Dromio, thou art my man, thou art thyself.

DROMIO OF SYRACUSE

I am an ass, I am a woman's man, and besides myself.

ANTIPHOLUS OF SYRACUSE

What woman's man? And how besides thyself?

DROMIO OF SYRACUSE

Marry, sir, besides myself, I am due to a woman; one that claims me, one that haunts me, one that will have me.

ANTIPHOLUS OF SYRACUSE

What claim lays she to thee?

DROMIO OF SYRACUSE

Marry, sir, such claim as you would lay to your horse; and she would have me as a beast: not that, I being a beast, she would have me; but that she, being a very beastly creature, lays claim to me.

ANTIPHOLUS OF SYRACUSE

What is she?

DROMIO OF SYRACUSE

A very reverent body; ay, such a one as a man may not speak of, without he say Sir-reverence.

I have but lean luck in the match, and yet is she
a wondrous fat marriage.

ANTIPHOLUS OF SYRACUSE

How dost thou mean a fat marriage?

DROMIO OF SYRACUSE

Marry, sir, she's the kitchen-wench, and all
grease; and I know not what use to put her
to, but to make a lamp of her, and run from
her by her own light. I warrant, her rags, and
the tallow in them, will burn a Poland winter.
If she lives till doomsday, she'll burn a week
longer than the whole world.

ANTIPHOLUS OF SYRACUSE

What complexion is she of?

DROMIO OF SYRACUSE

Swart, like my shoe, but her face nothing like
so clean kept. For why she sweats; a man may
go overshoes in the grime of it.

ANTIPHOLUS OF SYRACUSE

That's a fault that water will mend.

DROMIO OF SYRACUSE

No, sir, 'tis in grain; Noah's flood could not
do it.

ANTIPHOLUS OF SYRACUSE

What's her name?

DROMIO OF SYRACUSE

Nell, sir; but her name and three quarters, that's

an ell and three quarters, will not measure her
from hip to hip.

ANTIPHOLUS OF SYRACUSE

Then she bears some breadth?

DROMIO OF SYRACUSE

No longer from head to foot than from hip to
hip. She is spherical, like a globe; I could find
out countries in her.

ANTIPHOLUS OF SYRACUSE

In what part of her body stands Ireland?

DROMIO OF SYRACUSE

Marry, sir, in her buttocks. I found it out by
the bogs.

ANTIPHOLUS OF SYRACUSE

Where Scotland?

DROMIO OF SYRACUSE

I found it by the barrenness; hard in the palm
of the hand.

ANTIPHOLUS OF SYRACUSE

Where France?

DROMIO OF SYRACUSE

In her forehead; armed and reverted, making
war against her heir.

ANTIPHOLUS OF SYRACUSE

Where England?

DROMIO OF SYRACUSE

I looked for the chalky cliffs, but I could find

no whiteness in them; but I guess it stood in her chin, by the salt rheum that ran between France and it.

ANTIPHOLUS OF SYRACUSE

Where Spain?

DROMIO OF SYRACUSE

Faith, I saw it not; but I felt it hot in her breath.

ANTIPHOLUS OF SYRACUSE

Where America, the Indies?

DROMIO OF SYRACUSE

Oh, sir, upon her nose, all o'er embellished with rubies, carbuncles, sapphires, declining their rich aspect to the hot breath of Spain; who sent whole armadoes of caracks to be ballast at her nose.

ANTIPHOLUS OF SYRACUSE

Where stood Belgia, the Netherlands?

DROMIO OF SYRACUSE

Oh, sir, I did not look so low. To conclude, this drudge, or diviner, laid claim to me; called me Dromio; swore I was assured to her; told me what privy marks I had about me, as, the mark of my shoulder, the mole in my neck, the great wart on my left arm, that I, amazed, ran from her as a witch.

And, I think, if my breast had not been made of faith, and my heart of steel,

She had transform'd me to a curtal dog, and
made me turn i' the wheel.

ANTIPHOLUS OF SYRACUSE

Go hie thee presently, post to the road.
An if the wind blow any way from shore,
I will not harbour in this town to-night.
If any bark put forth, come to the mart,
Where I will walk till thou return to me.
If every one knows us, and we know none,
'Tis time, I think, to trudge, pack, and be gone.

DROMIO OF SYRACUSE

As from a bear a man would run for life,
So fly I from her that would be my wife.

Exit

ANTIPHOLUS OF SYRACUSE

There's none but witches do inhabit here;
And therefore 'tis high time that I were hence.
She that doth call me husband, even my soul
Doth for a wife abhor. But her fair sister,
Possess'd with such a gentle sovereign grace,
Of such enchanting presence and discourse,
Hath almost made me traitor to myself.
But, lest myself be guilty to self-wrong,
I'll stop mine ears against the mermaid's song.

Enter ANGELO *with the chain*

ANGELO

Master Antipholus—

ANTIPHOLUS OF SYRACUSE

Ay, that's my name.

ANGELO

I know it well, sir. Lo, here is the chain.

I thought to have ta'en you at the Porpentine.

The chain unfinish'd made me stay thus long.

ANTIPHOLUS OF SYRACUSE

What is your will that I shall do with this?

ANGELO

What please yourself, sir. I have made it for you.

ANTIPHOLUS OF SYRACUSE

Made it for me, sir! I bespoke it not.

ANGELO

Not once, nor twice, but twenty times you have.

Go home with it, and please your wife withal;

And soon at supper-time I'll visit you,

And then receive my money for the chain.

ANTIPHOLUS OF SYRACUSE

I pray you, sir, receive the money now,

For fear you ne'er see chain nor money more.

ANGELO

You are a merry man, sir. Fare you well.

Exit

ANTIPHOLUS OF SYRACUSE

What I should think of this, I cannot tell.

But this I think, there's no man is so vain

That would refuse so fair an offer'd chain.
I see a man here needs not live by shifts,
When in the streets he meets such golden gifts.
I'll to the mart, and there for Dromio stay;
If any ship put out, then straight away.

Exit

Act IV

SCENE I. A PUBLIC PLACE

Enter Second Merchant, ANGELO, *and an* Officer

SECOND MERCHANT

You know since Pentecost the sum is due,
And since I have not much importuned you;
Nor now I had not, but that I am bound
To Persia, and want guilders for my voyage.
Therefore make present satisfaction,
Or I'll attach you by this officer.

ANGELO

Even just the sum that I do owe to you
Is growing to me by Antipholus;
And in the instant that I met with you
He had of me a chain. At five o'clock
I shall receive the money for the same.
Pleaseth you walk with me down to his house,
I will discharge my bond, and thank you too.

Enter ANTIPHOLUS *of*
Ephesus *and* DROMIO *of* Ephesus
from the courtesan's

OFFICER

That labour may you save. See where he comes.

ANTIPHOLUS OF EPHESUS

While I go to the goldsmith's house, go thou
And buy a rope's end; that will I bestow
Among my wife and her confederates,
For locking me out of my doors by day.
But, soft! I see the goldsmith. Get thee gone;
Buy thou a rope, and bring it home to me.

DROMIO OF EPHESUS

I buy a thousand pound a year, I buy a rope.

Exit

ANTIPHOLUS OF EPHESUS

A man is well holp up that trusts to you.
I promised your presence and the chain;
But neither chain nor goldsmith came to me.
Belike you thought our love would last too long,
If it were chain'd together, and therefore came
not.

ANGELO

Saving your merry humour, here's the note
How much your chain weighs to the utmost
carat,
The fineness of the gold, and chargeful fashion,

68

Which doth amount to three odd ducats more
Than I stand debted to this gentleman.
I pray you, see him presently discharged,
For he is bound to sea, and stays but for it.

ANTIPHOLUS OF EPHESUS

I am not furnish'd with the present money;
Besides, I have some business in the town.
Good signior, take the stranger to my house,
And with you take the chain, and bid my wife
Disburse the sum on the receipt thereof.
Perchance I will be there as soon as you.

ANGELO

Then you will bring the chain to her yourself?

ANTIPHOLUS OF EPHESUS

No; bear it with you, lest I come not time
enough.

ANGELO

Well, sir, I will. Have you the chain about you?

ANTIPHOLUS OF EPHESUS

An if I have not, sir, I hope you have;
Or else you may return without your money.

ANGELO

Nay, come, I pray you, sir, give me the chain.
Both wind and tide stays for this gentleman,
And I, to blame, have held him here too long.

ANTIPHOLUS OF EPHESUS

Good Lord! You use this dalliance to excuse

Your breach of promise to the Porpentine.
I should have chid you for not bringing it,
But, like a shrew, you first begin to brawl.

SECOND MERCHANT

The hour steals on; I pray you, sir, dispatch.

ANGELO

You hear how he importunes me; the chain!

ANTIPHOLUS OF EPHESUS

Why, give it to my wife, and fetch your money.

ANGELO

Come, come, you know I gave it you even now.
Either send the chain, or send me by some
token.

ANTIPHOLUS OF EPHESUS

Fie, now you run this humour out of breath.
Come, where's the chain? I pray you, let me
see it.

SECOND MERCHANT

My business cannot brook this dalliance.
Good sir, say whether you'll answer me or no.
If not, I'll leave him to the officer.

ANTIPHOLUS OF EPHESUS

I answer you! what should I answer you?

ANGELO

The money that you owe me for the chain.

ANTIPHOLUS OF EPHESUS

I owe you none till I receive the chain.

ANGELO

    You know I gave it you half an hour since.

ANTIPHOLUS OF EPHESUS

    You gave me none. You wrong me much to
    say so.

ANGELO

    You wrong me more, sir, in denying it.

    Consider how it stands upon my credit.

SECOND MERCHANT

    Well, officer, arrest him at my suit.

OFFICER

    I do; and charge you in the Duke's name to
    obey me.

ANGELO

    This touches me in reputation.

    Either consent to pay this sum for me,

    Or I attach you by this officer.

ANTIPHOLUS OF EPHESUS

    Consent to pay thee that I never had!

    Arrest me, foolish fellow, if thou darest.

ANGELO

    Here is thy fee; arrest him, officer.

    I would not spare my brother in this case,

    If he should scorn me so apparently.

OFFICER

    I do arrest you, sir. You hear the suit.

ANTIPHOLUS OF EPHESUS

I do obey thee till I give thee bail.

But, sirrah, you shall buy this sport as dear

As all the metal in your shop will answer.

ANGELO

Sir, sir, I shall have law in Ephesus,

To your notorious shame; I doubt it not.

Enter DROMIO *of Syracuse,*

from the bay

DROMIO OF SYRACUSE

Master, there is a bark of Epidamnum

That stays but till her owner comes aboard,

And then, sir, she bears away. Our fraughtage, sir,

I have convey'd aboard; and I have bought

The oil, the balsamum, and aqua-vitae.

The ship is in her trim; the merry wind

Blows fair from land. They stay for nought at

all

But for their owner, master, and yourself.

ANTIPHOLUS OF EPHESUS

How now! A madman! Why, thou peevish sheep,

What ship of Epidamnum stays for me?

DROMIO OF SYRACUSE

A ship you sent me to, to hire waftage.

ANTIPHOLUS OF EPHESUS

Thou drunken slave, I sent thee for a rope,

And told thee to what purpose and what end.

DROMIO OF SYRACUSE

> You sent me for a rope's end as soon.
>
> You sent me to the bay, sir, for a bark.

ANTIPHOLUS OF EPHESUS

> I will debate this matter at more leisure,
>
> And teach your ears to list me with more heed.
>
> To Adriana, villain, hie thee straight.
>
> Give her this key, and tell her, in the desk
>
> That's cover'd o'er with Turkish tapestry
>
> There is a purse of ducats; let her send it.
>
> Tell her I am arrested in the street,
>
> And that shall bail me. Hie thee, slave, be gone!
>
> On, officer, to prison till it come.

> > > *Exeunt Second Merchant,*
> > >
> > > *Angelo, Officer, and*
> > >
> > > ANTIPHOLUS of Ephesus

DROMIO OF SYRACUSE

> To Adriana! that is where we dined,
>
> Where Dowsabel did claim me for her husband.
>
> She is too big, I hope, for me to compass.
>
> Thither I must, although against my will,
>
> For servants must their masters' minds fulfil.

> > > *Exit*

SCENE II. THE HOUSE OF ANTIPHOLUS OF EPHESUS

Enter ADRIANA *and* LUCIANA

ADRIANA

 Ah, Luciana, did he tempt thee so?
 Mightst thou perceive austerely in his eye
 That he did plead in earnest, yea or no?
 Look'd he or red or pale, or sad or merrily?
 What observation madest thou, in this case,
 Of his heart's meteors tilting in his face?

LUCIANA

 First he denied you had in him no right.

ADRIANA

 He meant he did me none; the more my spite.

LUCIANA

 Then swore he that he was a stranger here.

ADRIANA

 And true he swore, though yet forsworn he were.

LUCIANA

 Then pleaded I for you.

ADRIANA

 And what said he?

LUCIANA

 That love I begg'd for you he begg'd of me.

ADRIANA

With what persuasion did he tempt thy love?

LUCIANA

With words that in an honest suit might move.

First he did praise my beauty, then my speech.

ADRIANA

Didst speak him fair?

LUCIANA

Have patience, I beseech.

ADRIANA

I cannot, nor I will not, hold me still;

My tongue, though not my heart, shall have his
will.

He is deformed, crooked, old, and sere,

Ill-faced, worse bodied, shapeless everywhere;

Vicious, ungentle, foolish, blunt, unkind;

Stigmatical in making, worse in mind.

LUCIANA

Who would be jealous, then, of such a one?

No evil lost is wail'd when it is gone.

ADRIANA

Ah, but I think him better than I say,

And yet would herein others' eyes were worse.

Far from her nest the lapwing cries away.

My heart prays for him, though my tongue do
curse.

Enter DROMIO of Syracuse

DROMIO OF SYRACUSE

Here! go; the desk, the purse! sweet, now, make
haste.

LUCIANA

How hast thou lost thy breath?

DROMIO OF SYRACUSE

By running fast.

ADRIANA

Where is thy master, Dromio? Is he well?

DROMIO OF SYRACUSE

No, he's in Tartar limbo, worse than hell.
A devil in an everlasting garment hath him;
One whose hard heart is button'd up with steel;
A fiend, a fury, pitiless and rough;
A wolf, nay, worse; a fellow all in buff;
A back-friend, a shoulder-clapper, one that
countermands
The passages of alleys, creeks, and narrow
lands;
A hound that runs counter, and yet draws dry-
foot well;
One that, before the Judgment, carries poor souls
to hell.

ADRIANA

Why, man, what is the matter?

DROMIO OF SYRACUSE

I do not know the matter, he is 'rested on the
case.

ADRIANA

What, is he arrested? Tell me at whose suit.

DROMIO OF SYRACUSE

I know not at whose suit he is arrested well;
But he's in a suit of buff which 'rested him, that
can I tell.
Will you send him, mistress, redemption, the
money in his desk?

ADRIANA

Go fetch it, sister. [*Exit Luciana*] This I wonder at,
That he, unknown to me, should be in debt.
Tell me, was he arrested on a band?

DROMIO OF SYRACUSE

Not on a band, but on a stronger thing;
A chain, a chain! Do you not hear it ring?

ADRIANA

What, the chain?

DROMIO OF SYRACUSE

No, no, the bell. 'Tis time that I were gone.
It was two ere I left him, and now the clock
strikes one.

ADRIANA

The hours come back—that did I never hear.

DROMIO OF SYRACUSE

O, yes; if any hour meet a sergeant, 'a turns back for very fear.

ADRIANA

As if Time were in debt! How fondly dost thou reason!

DROMIO OF SYRACUSE

Time is a very bankrupt, and owes more than
he's worth to season.

Nay, he's a thief too. Have you not heard men
say,

That Time comes stealing on by night and day?

If Time be in debt and theft, and a sergeant in
the way,

Hath he not reason to turn back an hour in a
day?

Re-enter LUCIANA *with a purse*

ADRIANA

Go, Dromio; there's the money, bear it straight;

And bring thy master home immediately.

Come, sister, I am press'd down with conceit—

Conceit, my comfort and my injury.

Exeunt

SCENE III. A PUBLIC PLACE

Enter ANTIPHOLUS of Syracuse

ANTIPHOLUS OF SYRACUSE

    There's not a man I meet but doth salute me

    As if I were their well-acquainted friend;

    And every one doth call me by my name.

    Some tender money to me; some invite me;

    Some other give me thanks for kindnesses;

    Some offer me commodities to buy;

    Even now a tailor call'd me in his shop,

    And show'd me silks that he had bought for
        me,

    And therewithal took measure of my body.

    Sure, these are but imaginary wiles,

    And Lapland sorcerers inhabit here.

           Enter DROMIO of Syracuse

DROMIO OF SYRACUSE

    Master, here's the gold you sent me for.—

    What, have you got the picture of old Adam
        new-apparelled?

ANTIPHOLUS OF SYRACUSE

    What gold is this? What Adam dost thou
    mean?

DROMIO OF SYRACUSE

    Not that Adam that kept the Paradise, but that
    Adam that keeps the prison. He that goes in

the calf's skin that was killed for the Prodigal; he that came behind you, sir, like an evil angel, and bid you forsake your liberty.

ANTIPHOLUS OF SYRACUSE

I understand thee not.

DROMIO OF SYRACUSE

No? Why, 'tis a plain case: he that went, like a base-viol, in a case of leather; the man, sir, that, when gentlemen are tired, gives them a sob, and 'rests them; he, sir, that takes pity on decayed men, and gives them suits of durance; he that sets up his rest to do more exploits with his mace than a morris-pike.

ANTIPHOLUS OF SYRACUSE

What, thou meanest an officer?

DROMIO OF SYRACUSE

Ay, sir, the sergeant of the band; he that brings any man to answer it that breaks his band; one that thinks a man always going to bed, and says, 'God give you good rest!'

ANTIPHOLUS OF SYRACUSE

Well, sir, there rest in your foolery. Is there any ship puts forth to-night? May we be gone?

DROMIO OF SYRACUSE

Why, sir, I brought you word an hour since, that the bark *Expedition* put forth to-night; and then were you hindered by the sergeant, to

tarry for the hoy *Delay*. Here are the angels that
you sent for to deliver you.

ANTIPHOLUS OF SYRACUSE

The fellow is distract, and so am I;

And here we wander in illusions.

Some blessed power deliver us from hence!

Enter a Courtesan

COURTESAN

Well met, well met, Master Antipholus.

I see, sir, you have found the goldsmith now.

Is that the chain you promised me to-day?

ANTIPHOLUS OF SYRACUSE

Satan, avoid! I charge thee, tempt me not.

DROMIO OF SYRACUSE

Master, is this Mistress Satan?

ANTIPHOLUS OF SYRACUSE

It is the devil.

DROMIO OF SYRACUSE

Nay, she is worse, she is the devil's dam; and
here she comes in the habit of a light wench;
and thereof comes that the wenches say, 'God
damn me;' that's as much to say, 'God make
me a light wench.' It is written, they appear to
men like angels of light. Light is an effect of
fire, and fire will burn; ergo, light wenches will
burn. Come not near her.

COURTESAN

Your man and you are marvellous merry, sir.
Will you go with me? We'll mend our dinner here?

DROMIO OF SYRACUSE

Master, if you do, expect spoon-meat; or bespeak a long spoon.

ANTIPHOLUS OF SYRACUSE

Why, Dromio?

DROMIO OF SYRACUSE

Marry, he must have a long spoon that must eat with the devil.

ANTIPHOLUS OF SYRACUSE

Avoid then, fiend! what tell'st thou me of supping?
Thou art, as you are all, a sorceress.
I conjure thee to leave me and be gone.

COURTESAN

Give me the ring of mine you had at dinner,
Or, for my diamond, the chain you promised,
And I'll be gone, sir, and not trouble you.

DROMIO OF SYRACUSE

Some devils ask but the parings of one's nail,
A rush, a hair, a drop of blood, a pin,
A nut, a cherry-stone;
But she, more covetous, would have a chain.
Master, be wise; an if you give it her,

The devil will shake her chain, and fright us
　　with it.

COURTESAN

　　I pray you, sir, my ring, or else the chain!

　　I hope you do not mean to cheat me so.

ANTIPHOLUS OF SYRACUSE

　　Avaunt, thou witch!—Come, Dromio, let us
　　go.

DROMIO OF SYRACUSE

　　'Fly pride,' says the peacock. Mistress, that you
　　know.

Exeunt
ANTIPHOLUS of Syracuse
and DROMIO of Syracuse

COURTESAN

　　Now, out of doubt Antipholus is mad,

　　Else would he never so demean himself.

　　A ring he hath of mine worth forty ducats,

　　And for the same he promised me a chain.

　　Both one and other he denies me now.

　　The reason that I gather he is mad,

　　Besides this present instance of his rage,

　　Is a mad tale he told to-day at dinner,

　　Of his own doors being shut against his
　　　entrance.

　　Belike his wife, acquainted with his fits,

　　On purpose shut the doors against his way.

My way is now to his home to his house,
And tell his wife that, being lunatic,
He rush'd into my house, and took perforce
My ring away. This course I fittest choose;
For forty ducats is too much to lose.

Exit

SCENE IV. A STREET

Enter ANTIPHOLUS *of Ephesus and the* Officer
ANTIPHOLUS OF EPHESUS

Fear me not, man; I will not break away.
I'll give thee, ere I leave thee, so much money,
To warrant thee, as I am 'rested for.
My wife is in a wayward mood to-day,
And will not lightly trust the messenger.
That I should be attach'd in Ephesus,
I tell you, 'twill sound harshly in her ears.

Enter DROMIO *of Ephesus*
with a rope's end

Here comes my man; I think he brings the
money.
How now, sir! have you that I sent you for?

DROMIO OF EPHESUS

Here's that, I warrant you, will pay them all.

ANTIPHOLUS OF EPHESUS

But where's the money?

DROMIO OF EPHESUS

Why, sir, I gave the money for the rope.

ANTIPHOLUS OF EPHESUS

Five hundred ducats, villain, for a rope?

DROMIO OF EPHESUS

I'll serve you, sir, five hundred at the rate.

ANTIPHOLUS OF EPHESUS

To what end did I bid thee hie thee home?

DROMIO OF EPHESUS

To a rope's end, sir; and to that end am I returned.

ANTIPHOLUS OF EPHESUS

And to that end, sir, I will welcome you.

Beating him

OFFICER

Good sir, be patient.

DROMIO OF EPHESUS

Nay, 'tis for me to be patient; I am in adversity.

OFFICER

Good, now, hold thy tongue.

DROMIO OF EPHESUS

Nay, rather persuade him to hold his hands.

ANTIPHOLUS OF EPHESUS

Thou whoreson, senseless villain!

DROMIO OF EPHESUS

I would I were senseless, sir, that I might not feel your blows.

ANTIPHOLUS OF EPHESUS

Thou art sensible in nothing but blows, and so is an ass.

DROMIO OF EPHESUS

I am an ass, indeed; you may prove it by my long ears. I have served him from the hour of my nativity to this instant, and have nothing at his hands for my service but blows. When I am cold, he heats me with beating; when I am warm, he cools me with beating. I am waked with it when I sleep; raised with it when I sit; driven out of doors with it when I go from home; welcomed home with it when I return; nay, I bear it on my shoulders, as a beggar wont her brat; and, I think, when he hath lamed me, I shall beg with it from door to door.

ANTIPHOLUS OF EPHESUS

Come, go along; my wife is coming yonder.

Enter ADRIANA, LUCIANA,
the Courtesan, *and* PINCH

DROMIO OF EPHESUS

Mistress, 'respice finem,' respect your end; or rather, the prophecy like the parrot, 'beware the rope's end.'

ANTIPHOLUS OF EPHESUS

Wilt thou still talk?

Beating him

COURTESAN

How say you now? Is not your husband mad?

ADRIANA

His incivility confirms no less.

Good Doctor Pinch, you are a conjurer;

Establish him in his true sense again,

And I will please you what you will demand.

LUCIANA

Alas, how fiery and how sharp he looks!

COURTESAN

Mark how he trembles in his ecstasy!

PINCH

Give me your hand, and let me feel your pulse.

ANTIPHOLUS OF EPHESUS

There is my hand, and let it feel your ear.

Striking him

PINCH

I charge thee, Satan, housed within this man,

To yield possession to my holy prayers,

And to thy state of darkness his thee straight.

I conjure thee by all the saints in heaven!

ANTIPHOLUS OF EPHESUS

Peace, doting wizard, peace! I am not mad.

ADRIANA

O, that thou wert not, poor distressed soul!

ANTIPHOLUS OF EPHESUS

You minion, you, are these your customers?

Did this companion with the saffron face
Revel and feast it at my house to-day,
Whilst upon me the guilty doors were shut,
And I denied to enter in my house?

ADRIANA

O husband, God doth know you dined at home;
Where would you had remain'd until this time,
Free from these slanders and this open shame!

ANTIPHOLUS OF EPHESUS

Dined at home! Thou villain, what sayest thou?

DROMIO OF EPHESUS

Sir, sooth to say, you did not dine at home.

ANTIPHOLUS OF EPHESUS

Were not my doors lock'd up, and I shut out?

DROMIO OF EPHESUS

Perdie, your doors were lock'd, and you shut out.

ANTIPHOLUS OF EPHESUS

And did not she herself revile me there?

DROMIO OF EPHESUS

Sans fable, she herself reviled you there.

ANTIPHOLUS OF EPHESUS

Did not her kitchen-maid rail, taunt, and
scorn me?

DROMIO OF EPHESUS

Certes, she did; the kitchen-vestal scorn'd you.

ANTIPHOLUS OF EPHESUS

And did not I in rage depart from thence?

DROMIO OF EPHESUS

In verity you did; my bones bear witness,
That since have felt the vigour of his rage.

ADRIANA

Is't good to soothe him in these contraries?

PINCH

It is no shame. The fellow finds his vein,
And, yielding to him, humours well his frenzy.

ANTIPHOLUS OF EPHESUS

Thou hast suborn'd the goldsmith to arrest me.

ADRIANA

Alas, I sent you money to redeem you,
By Dromio here, who came in haste for it.

DROMIO OF EPHESUS

Money by me! heart and good-will you might;
But surely, master, not a rag of money.

ANTIPHOLUS OF EPHESUS

Went'st not thou to her for a purse of ducats?

ADRIANA

He came to me, and I deliver'd it.

LUCIANA

And I am witness with her that she did.

DROMIO OF EPHESUS

God and the rope-maker bear me witness
That I was sent for nothing but a rope!

PINCH

Mistress, both man and master is possess'd;

I know it by their pale and deadly looks.

They must be bound, and laid in some dark room.

ANTIPHOLUS OF EPHESUS

Say, wherefore didst them lock me forth to-day?

And why dost thou deny the bag of gold?

ADRIANA

I did not, gentle husband, lock thee forth.

DROMIO OF EPHESUS

And, gentle master, I received no gold;

But I confess, sir, that we were lock'd out.

ADRIANA

Dissembling villain, them speak'st false in both.

ANTIPHOLUS OF EPHESUS

Dissembling harlot, them art false in all,

And art confederate with a damned pack

To make a loathsome abject scorn of me.

But with these nails I'll pluck out these false eyes,

That would behold in me this shameful sport.

Enter three or four, and offer to bind him.

He strives.

ADRIANA

O, bind him, bind him! let him not come near me.

PINCH

More company! The fiend is strong within him.

LUCIANA

Ay me, poor man, how pale and wan he looks!

ANTIPHOLUS OF EPHESUS

What, will you murder me? Thou gaoler, thou,

I am thy prisoner: wilt thou suffer them

To make a rescue?

OFFICER

Masters, let him go.

He is my prisoner, and you shall not have him.

PINCH

Go bind this man, for he is frantic too.

They offer to bind

DROMIO of Ephesus

ADRIANA

What wilt thou do, thou peevish officer?

Hast thou delight to see a wretched man

Do outrage and displeasure to himself?

OFFICER

He is my prisoner. If I let him go,

The debt he owes will be required of me.

ADRIANA

I will discharge thee ere I go from thee.

Bear me forthwith unto his creditor,

And, knowing how the debt grows, I will pay it.

Good master doctor, see him safe convey'd

Home to my house. O most unhappy day!

ANTIPHOLUS OF EPHESUS

O most unhappy strumpet!

DROMIO OF EPHESUS

Master, I am here entered in bond for you.

ANTIPHOLUS OF EPHESUS

Out on thee, villain! wherefore dost thou
mad me?

DROMIO OF EPHESUS

Will you be bound for nothing? Be mad, good
master: cry, 'the devil!'

LUCIANA

God help, poor souls, how idly do they talk!

ADRIANA

Go bear him hence. Sister, go you with me.

Exeunt all but Adriana,
Luciana, Officer and Courtesan

Say now; whose suit is he arrested at?

OFFICER

One Angelo, a goldsmith. Do you know him?

ADRIANA

I know the man. What is the sum he owes?

OFFICER

Two hundred ducats.

ADRIANA

Say, how grows it due?

OFFICER

Due for a chain your husband had of him.

ADRIANA

He did bespeak a chain for me, but had it not.

COURTESAN

When as your husband, all in rage, to-day

Came to my house, and took away my ring,

The ring I saw upon his finger now,

Straight after did I meet him with a chain.

ADRIANA

It may be so, but I did never see it.

Come, gaoler, bring me where the goldsmith is.

I long to know the truth hereof at large.

Enter ANTIPHOLUS *of*
Syracuse *with his rapier drawn, and*
DROMIO *of* Syracuse

LUCIANA

God, for thy mercy! they are loose again.

ADRIANA

And come with naked swords.

Let's call more help to have them bound again.

OFFICER

Away! they'll kill us.

Exeunt all but
ANTIPHOLUS *of* Syracuse
and DROMIO *of* Syracuse

ANTIPHOLUS OF SYRACUSE

I see these witches are afraid of swords.

DROMIO OF SYRACUSE

She that would be your wife now ran from you.

ANTIPHOLUS OF SYRACUSE

Come to the Centaur; fetch our stuff from thence.

I long that we were safe and sound aboard.

DROMIO OF SYRACUSE

Faith, stay here this night; they will surely do us no harm. You saw they speak us fair, give us gold. Methinks they are such a gentle nation, that, but for the mountain of mad flesh that claims marriage of me, I could find in my heart to stay here still, and turn witch.

ANTIPHOLUS OF SYRACUSE

I will not stay to-night for all the town;

Therefore away, to get our stuff aboard.

Exeunt

Act V

SCENE I. A STREET BEFORE A PRIORY

Enter Second Merchant *and* ANGELO

ANGELO

    I am sorry, sir, that I have hinder'd you;

    But, I protest, he had the chain of me,

    Though most dishonestly he doth deny it.

SECOND MERCHANT

    How is the man esteem'd here in the city?

ANGELO

    Of very reverent reputation, sir,

    Of credit infinite, highly beloved,

    Second to none that lives here in the city.

    His word might bear my wealth at any time.

SECOND MERCHANT

    Speak softly. Yonder, as I think, he walks.

        Enter ANTIPHOLUS *of Syracuse*

        and DROMIO *of Syracuse*

ANGELO

'Tis so; and that self chain about his neck,
Which he forswore most monstrously to have.
Good sir, draw near to me, I'll speak to him;
Signior Antipholus, I wonder much
That you would put me to this shame and
trouble;
And, not without some scandal to yourself,
With circumstance and oaths so to deny
This chain which now you wear so openly.
Beside the charge, the shame, imprisonment,
You have done wrong to this my honest friend;
Who, but for staying on our controversy,
Had hoisted sail and put to sea to-day.
This chain you had of me; can you deny it?

ANTIPHOLUS OF SYRACUSE

I think I had; I never did deny it.

SECOND MERCHANT

Yes, that you did, sir, and forswore it too.

ANTIPHOLUS OF SYRACUSE

Who heard me to deny it or forswear it?

SECOND MERCHANT

These ears of mine, thou know'st, did hear thee.
Fie on thee, wretch! 'tis pity that thou livest
To walk where any honest men resort.

ANTIPHOLUS OF SYRACUSE

Thou art a villain to impeach me thus.

I'll prove mine honour and mine honesty
Against thee presently, if thou darest stand.

SECOND MERCHANT

I dare, and do defy thee for a villain. *They draw.*

Enter ADRIANA, LUCIANA,
the Courtesan, *and others*

ADRIANA

Hold, hurt him not, for God's sake! he is mad.
Some get within him, take his sword away.
Bind Dromio too, and bear them to my house.

DROMIO OF SYRACUSE

Run, master, run; for God's sake, take a house!
This is some priory. In, or we are spoil'd!

Exeunt
ANTIPHOLUS of Syracuse
and DROMIO of Syracuse
to the Priory

Enter the Lady Abbess

ABBESS

Be quiet, people. Wherefore throng you hither?

ADRIANA

To fetch my poor distracted husband hence.
Let us come in, that we may bind him fast,
And bear him home for his recovery.

ANGELO

I knew he was not in his perfect wits.

SECOND MERCHANT

I am sorry now that I did draw on him.

ABBESS

How long hath this possession held the man?

ADRIANA

This week he hath been heavy, sour, sad,
And much different from the man he was;
But till this afternoon his passion
Ne'er brake into extremity of rage.

ABBESS

Hath he not lost much wealth by wreck of sea?
Buried some dear friend? Hath not else his eye
Stray'd his affection in unlawful love?
A sin prevailing much in youthful men,
Who give their eyes the liberty of gazing.
Which of these sorrows is he subject to?

ADRIANA

To none of these, except it be the last;
Namely, some love that drew him oft from
home.

ABBESS

You should for that have reprehended him.

ADRIANA

Why, so I did.

ABBESS

Ay, but not rough enough.

ADRIANA

As roughly as my modesty would let me.

ABBESS

Haply, in private.

ADRIANA

And in assemblies too.

ABBESS

Ay, but not enough.

ADRIANA

It was the copy of our conference.

In bed, he slept not for my urging it;

At board, he fed not for my urging it;

Alone, it was the subject of my theme;

In company I often glanced it;

Still did I tell him it was vile and bad.

ABBESS

And thereof came it that the man was mad.

The venom clamours of a jealous woman,

Poisons more deadly than a mad dog's tooth.

It seems his sleeps were hinder'd by thy railing,

And thereof comes it that his head is light.

Thou say'st his meat was sauced with thy upbraidings.

Unquiet meals make ill digestions;

Thereof the raging fire of fever bred;

And what's a fever but a fit of madness?

Thou say'st his sports were hinder'd by thy brawls.
Sweet recreation barr'd, what doth ensue
But moody and dull melancholy,
Kinsman to grim and comfortless despair;
And at her heels a huge infectious troop
Of pale distemperatures and foes to life?
In food, in sport, and life-preserving rest
To be disturb'd, would mad or man or beast.
The consequence is, then, thy jealous fits
Have scared thy husband from the use of wits.

LUCIANA

She never reprehended him but mildly,
When he demean'd himself rough, rude, and
    wildly.

Why bear you these rebukes, and answer not?

ADRIANA

She did betray me to my own reproof.

Good people, enter, and lay hold on him.

ABBESS

No, not a creature enters in my house.

ADRIANA

Then let your servants bring my husband forth.

ABBESS

Neither. He took this place for sanctuary,
And it shall privilege him from your hands
Till I have brought him to his wits again,
Or lose my labour in assaying it.

ADRIANA

>I will attend my husband, be his nurse,
>Diet his sickness, for it is my office,
>And will have no attorney but myself;
>And therefore let me have him home with me.

ABBESS

>Be patient; for I will not let him stir
>Till I have used the approved means I have,
>With wholesome syrups, drugs and holy prayers,
>To make of him a formal man again.
>It is a branch and parcel of mine oath,
>A charitable duty of my order.
>Therefore depart, and leave him here with me.

ADRIANA

>I will not hence, and leave my husband here.
>And ill it doth beseem your holiness
>To separate the husband and the wife.

ABBESS

>Be quiet, and depart. Thou shalt not have him.

Exit

LUCIANA

>Complain unto the Duke of this indignity.

ADRIANA

>Come, go. I will fall prostrate at his feet,
>And never rise until my tears and prayers
>Have won his Grace to come in person hither,
>And take perforce my husband from the abbess.

SECOND MERCHANT

> By this, I think, the dial points at five.
> Anon, I'm sure, the Duke himself in person
> Comes this way to the melancholy vale,
> The place of death and sorry execution,
> Behind the ditches of the abbey here.

ANGELO

> Upon what cause?

SECOND MERCHANT

> To see a reverend Syracusian merchant,
> Who put unluckily into this bay
> Against the laws and statutes of this town,
> Beheaded publicly for his offence.

ANGELO

> See where they come. We will behold his death.

LUCIANA

> Kneel to the Duke before he pass the abbey.

> *Enter* DUKE, *attended;*
> AEGEON *bareheaded; with the* Headsman
> *and other* Officers

DUKE

> Yet once again proclaim it publicly,
> If any friend will pay the sum for him,
> He shall not die; so much we tender him.

ADRIANA

> Justice, most sacred Duke, against the abbess!

DUKE

> She is a virtuous and a reverend lady.
>
> It cannot be that she hath done thee wrong.

ADRIANA

> May it please your Grace, Antipholus my
> husband,
>
> Whom I made lord of me and all I had,
>
> At your important letters, this ill day
>
> A most outrageous fit of madness took him;
>
> That desperately he hurried through the street,
>
> With him his bondman, all as mad as he,
>
> Doing displeasure to the citizens
>
> By rushing in their houses, bearing thence
>
> Rings, jewels, any thing his rage did like.
>
> Once did I get him bound, and sent him home,
>
> Whilst to take order for the wrongs I went,
>
> That here and there his fury had committed.
>
> Anon, I wot not by what strong escape,
>
> He broke from those that had the guard of him;
>
> And with his mad attendant and himself,
>
> Each one with ireful passion, with drawn
> swords,
>
> Met us again, and, madly bent on us,
>
> Chased us away; till, raising of more aid,
>
> We came again to bind them. Then they fled
>
> Into this abbey, whither we pursued them;

And here the abbess shuts the gates on us,
And will not suffer us to fetch him out,
Nor send him forth, that we may bear him
hence.
Therefore, most gracious Duke, with thy
command
Let him be brought forth, and borne hence for
help.

DUKE

Long since thy husband served me in my wars;
And I to thee engaged a prince's word,
When thou didst make him master of thy bed,
To do him all the grace and good I could.
Go, some of you, knock at the abbey-gate,
And bid the lady abbess come to me.
I will determine this before I stir.

Enter a Servant

SERVANT

O mistress, mistress, shift and save yourself!
My master and his man are both broke loose,
Beaten the maids a-row, and bound the doctor,
Whose beard they have singed off with brands
of fire;
And ever, as it blazed, they threw on him
Great pails of puddled mire to quench the hair.
My master preaches patience to him, and the
while

His man with scissors nicks him like a fool;
And sure, unless you send some present help,
Between them they will kill the conjurer.

ADRIANA

Peace, fool! thy master and his man are here;
And that is false thou dost report to us.

SERVANT

Mistress, upon my life, I tell you true;
I have not breathed almost since I did see it.
He cries for you, and vows, if he can take you,
To scorch your face and to disfigure you.

Cry within

Hark, hark! I hear him, mistress. Fly, be gone!

DUKE

Come, stand by me; fear nothing. Guard with
halberds!

ADRIANA

Ay me, it is my husband! Witness you,
That he is borne about invisible.
Even now we housed him in the abbey here;
And now he's there, past thought of human
reason.

Enter ANTIPHOLUS *of Ephesus and*
DROMIO *of Ephesus*

ANTIPHOLUS OF EPHESUS

Justice, most gracious Duke, O, grant me
justice!

Even for the service that long since I did thee,
When I bestrid thee in the wars, and took
Deep scars to save thy life; even for the blood
That then I lost for thee, now grant me justice.

AEGEON

Unless the fear of death doth make me dote,
I see my son Antipholus, and Dromio.

ANTIPHOLUS OF EPHESUS

Justice, sweet prince, against that woman there!
She whom thou gavest to me to be my wife,
That hath abused and dishonour'd me
Even in the strength and height of injury.
Beyond imagination is the wrong
That she this day hath shameless thrown on
    me.

DUKE

Discover how, and thou shalt find me just.

ANTIPHOLUS OF EPHESUS

This day, great Duke, she shut the doors upon
    me,
While she with harlots feasted in my house.

DUKE

A grievous fault! Say, woman, didst thou so?

ADRIANA

No, my good lord. Myself, he and my sister
To-day did dine together. So befal my soul
As this is false he burdens me withal!

LUCIANA

Ne'er may I look on day, nor sleep on night,
But she tells to your Highness simple truth!

ANGELO

O perjured woman! They are both forsworn.
In this the madman justly chargeth them.

ANTIPHOLUS OF EPHESUS

My liege, I am advised what I say;
Neither disturbed with the effect of wine,
Nor heady-rash, provoked with raging ire,
Albeit my wrongs might make one wiser mad.
This woman lock'd me out this day from dinner.
That goldsmith there, were he not pack'd with
  her,
Could witness it, for he was with me then;
Who parted with me to go fetch a chain,
Promising to bring it to the Porpentine,
Where Balthazar and I did dine together.
Our dinner done, and he not coming thither,
I went to seek him. In the street I met him,
And in his company that gentleman.
There did this perjured goldsmith swear me down
That I this day of him received the chain,
Which, God he knows, I saw not. For the which
He did arrest me with an officer.
I did obey; and sent my peasant home
For certain ducats. He with none return'd.

Then fairly I bespoke the officer
To go in person with me to my house.
By the way we met my wife, her sister, and a
    rabble more
Of vile confederates. Along with them
They brought one Pinch, a hungry lean-faced
    villain,
A mere anatomy, a mountebank,
A threadbare juggler, and a fortune-teller,
A needy, hollow-eyed, sharp-looking wretch,
A living-dead man. This pernicious slave,
Forsooth, took on him as a conjurer;
And, gazing in mine eyes, feeling my pulse,
And with no face, as 'twere, outfacing me,
Cries out, I was possess'd. Then all together
They fell upon me, bound me, bore me thence,
And in a dark and dankish vault at home
There left me and my man, both bound
    together;
Till, gnawing with my teeth my bonds in sunder,
I gain'd my freedom, and immediately
Ran hither to your Grace; whom I beseech
To give me ample satisfaction
For these deep shames and great indignities.

ANGELO

My lord, in truth, thus far I witness with him,
That he dined not at home, but was lock'd out.

DUKE

But had he such a chain of thee or no?

ANGELO

He had, my lord, and when he ran in here,

These people saw the chain about his neck.

SECOND MERCHANT

Besides, I will be sworn these ears of mine

Heard you confess you had the chain of him,

After you first forswore it on the mart,

And thereupon I drew my sword on you;

And then you fled into this abbey here,

From whence, I think, you are come by miracle.

ANTIPHOLUS OF EPHESUS

I never came within these abbey walls;

Nor ever didst thou draw thy sword on me.

I never saw the chain, so help me Heaven,

And this is false you burden me withal!

DUKE

Why, what an intricate impeach is this!

I think you all have drunk of Circe's cup.

If here you housed him, here he would have
    been;

If he were mad, he would not plead so coldly.

You say he dined at home; the goldsmith here

Denies that saying. Sirrah, what say you?

DROMIO OF EPHESUS

Sir, he dined with her there, at the Porpentine.

COURTESAN

He did; and from my finger snatch'd that ring.

ANTIPHOLUS OF EPHESUS

'Tis true, my liege; this ring I had of her.

DUKE

Saw'st thou him enter at the abbey here?

COURTESAN

As sure, my liege, as I do see your Grace.

DUKE

Why, this is strange. Go call the abbess hither.

I think you are all mated, or stark mad.

Exit one to the Abbess

AEGEON

Most mighty Duke, vouchsafe me speak a word.

Haply I see a friend will save my life,

And pay the sum that may deliver me.

DUKE

Speak freely, Syracusian, what thou wilt.

AEGEON

Is not your name, sir, call'd Antipholus?

And is not that your bondman, Dromio?

DROMIO OF EPHESUS

Within this hour I was his bondman, sir,

But he, I thank him, gnaw'd in two my cords.

Now am I Dromio, and his man unbound.

AEGEON

I am sure you both of you remember me.

DROMIO OF EPHESUS

    Ourselves we do remember, sir, by you;

    For lately we were bound, as you are now.

    You are not Pinch's patient, are you, sir?

AEGEON

    Why look you strange on me? You know me well.

ANTIPHOLUS OF EPHESUS

    I never saw you in my life till now.

AEGEON

    O, grief hath changed me since you saw me last,

    And careful hours with time's deformed hand

    Have written strange defeatures in my face.

    But tell me yet, dost thou not know my voice?

ANTIPHOLUS OF EPHESUS

    Neither.

AEGEON

    Dromio, nor thou?

DROMIO OF EPHESUS

    No, trust me, sir, nor I.

AEGEON

    I am sure thou dost.

DROMIO OF EPHESUS

    Ay, sir, but I am sure I do not; and whatsoever a

    man denies, you are now bound to believe him.

AEGEON

    Not know my voice! O time's extremity,

Hast thou so crack'd and splitted my poor
    tongue
In seven short years, that here my only son
Knows not my feeble key of untuned cares?
Though now this grained face of mine be hid
In sap-consuming winter's drizzled snow,
And all the conduits of my blood froze up,
Yet hath my night of life some memory,
My wasting lamps some fading glimmer left,
My dull deaf ears a little use to hear.
All these old witnesses—I cannot err—
Tell me thou art my son Antipholus.

ANTIPHOLUS OF EPHESUS

I never saw my father in my life.

AEGEON

But seven years since, in Syracusa, boy,
Thou know'st we parted. But perhaps, my son,
Thou shamest to acknowledge me in misery.

ANTIPHOLUS OF EPHESUS

The Duke and all that know me in the city
Can witness with me that it is not so.
I ne'er saw Syracusa in my life.

DUKE

I tell thee, Syracusian, twenty years
Have I been patron to Antipholus,
During which time he ne'er saw Syracusa.
I see thy age and dangers make thee dote.

Re-enter Abbess, *with*
ANTIPHOLUS of Syracuse *and*
DROMIO of Syracuse

ABBESS

Most mighty Duke, behold a man much wrong'd.

All gather to see them

ADRIANA

I see two husbands, or mine eyes deceive me.

DUKE

One of these men is Genius to the other;
And so of these. Which is the natural man,
And which the spirit? Who deciphers them?

DROMIO OF SYRACUSE

I, sir, am Dromio. Command him away.

DROMIO OF EPHESUS

I, sir, am Dromio. Pray, let me stay.

ANTIPHOLUS OF SYRACUSE

Aegeon art thou not? or else his ghost?

DROMIO OF SYRACUSE

O, my old master! who hath bound him here?

ABBESS

Whoever bound him, I will loose his bonds,
And gain a husband by his liberty.
Speak, old Aegeon, if thou be'st the man
That hadst a wife once call'd Aemilia,
That bore thee at a burden two fair sons.

O, if thou be'st the same Aegeon, speak,
And speak unto the same Aemilia!

AEGEON

If I dream not, thou art Aemilia.
If thou art she, tell me where is that son
That floated with thee on the fatal raft?

ABBESS

By men of Epidamnum he and I
And the twin Dromio, all were taken up;
But by and by rude fishermen of Corinth
By force took Dromio and my son from them,
And me they left with those of Epidamnum.
What then became of them I cannot tell;
I to this fortune that you see me in.

DUKE

Why, here begins his morning story right.
These two Antipholuses, these two so like,
And these two Dromios, one in semblance,
Besides her urging of her wreck at sea—
These are the parents to these children,
Which accidentally are met together.
Antipholus, thou camest from Corinth first?

ANTIPHOLUS OF SYRACUSE

No, sir, not I; I came from Syracuse.

DUKE

Stay, stand apart; I know not which is which.

ANTIPHOLUS OF EPHESUS

I came from Corinth, my most gracious lord.

DROMIO OF EPHESUS

And I with him.

ANTIPHOLUS OF EPHESUS

Brought to this town by that most famous warrior.

Duke Menaphon, your most renowned uncle.

ADRIANA

Which of you two did dine with me to-day?

ANTIPHOLUS OF SYRACUSE

I, gentle mistress.

ADRIANA

And are not you my husband?

ANTIPHOLUS OF EPHESUS

No; I say nay to that.

ANTIPHOLUS OF SYRACUSE

And so do I; yet did she call me so,

And this fair gentlewoman, her sister here,

Did call me brother. [*To Lucia*] What I told you
then,

I hope I shall have leisure to make good;

If this be not a dream I see and hear.

ANGELO

That is the chain, sir, which you had of me.

ANTIPHOLUS OF SYRACUSE

I think it be, sir; I deny it not.

ANTIPHOLUS OF EPHESUS

And you, sir, for this chain arrested me.

ANGELO

I think I did, sir; I deny it not.

ADRIANA

I sent you money, sir, to be your bail,

By Dromio; but I think he brought it not.

DROMIO OF EPHESUS

No, none by me.

ANTIPHOLUS OF SYRACUSE

This purse of ducats I received from you,

And Dromio my man did bring them me.

I see we still did meet each other's man;

And I was ta'en for him, and he for me;

And thereupon these ERRORS are arose.

ANTIPHOLUS OF EPHESUS

These ducats pawn I for my father here.

DUKE

It shall not need; thy father hath his life.

COURTESAN

Sir, I must have that diamond from you.

ANTIPHOLUS OF EPHESUS

There, take it; and much thanks for my good
cheer.

ABBESS

Renowned Duke, vouchsafe to take the pains

To go with us into the abbey here,

And hear at large discoursed all our fortunes;
And all that are assembled in this place,
That by this sympathized one day's error
Have suffer'd wrong, go keep us company,
And we shall make full satisfaction.
Thirty-three years have I but gone in travail
Of you, my sons; and till this present hour
My heavy burthen ne'er delivered.
The Duke, my husband, and my children both,
And you the calendars of their nativity,
Go to a gossips' feast, and go with me;
After so long grief, such nativity!

DUKE

With all my heart, I'll gossip at this feast.

Exeunt all but ANTIPHOLUS of
Syracuse, ANTIPHOLUS of
Ephesus, DROMIO of Syracuse,
and DROMIO of Ephesus

DROMIO OF SYRACUSE

Master, shall I fetch your stuff from ship-
board?

ANTIPHOLUS OF EPHESUS

Dromio, what stuff of mine hast thou
embark'd?

DROMIO OF SYRACUSE

Your goods that lay at host, sir, in the Centaur.

ANTIPHOLUS OF SYRACUSE

    He speaks to me—I am your master, Dromio!

    Come, go with us; we'll look to that anon.

    Embrace thy brother there; rejoice with him.

               Exeunt ANTIPHOLUS of Syracuse

                 and ANTIPHOLUS of Ephesus

DROMIO OF SYRACUSE

    There is a fat friend at your master's house,

    That kitchen'd me for you to-day at dinner.

    She now shall be my sister, not my wife.

DROMIO OF EPHESUS

    Methinks you are my glass, and not my brother.

    I see by you I am a sweet-faced youth.

    Will you walk in to see their gossiping?

DROMIO OF SYRACUSE

    Not I, sir; you are my elder.

DROMIO OF EPHESUS

    That's a question. How shall we try it?

DROMIO OF SYRACUSE

    We'll draw cuts for the senior. Till then lead thou
    first.

DROMIO OF EPHESUS

    Nay, then, thus:—

    We came into the world like brother and brother;

    And now let's go hand in hand, not one before
        another.

                            Exeunt